Mark-Napped!

Ellie Sipila

Illustrated by

Christina Brown

PELICAN PUBLISHING COMPANY
Gretna 2019

To everyone who has ever felt misunderstood, misplaced, or misused. You're not alone.

Library of Congress Cataloging-in-Publication Data

Names: Sipila, Ellie, author. | Brown, Christina (Illustrator), illustrator.
Title: Mark-napped! / Ellie Sipila ; illustrated by Christina Brown.
Description: Gretna : Pelican Publishing Company, 2019. | Summary: Invites the reader to act as Sidekick to an investigator who interrogates all of the punctuation marks present when Comma disappeared from the playground at recess. Includes facts about conjunctions, clauses, contractions, quotation marks, and more.
Identifiers: LCCN 2018041572| ISBN 9781455624638 (pbk. : alk. paper) | ISBN 9781455624645 (ebook)
Subjects: | CYAC: Punctuation—Fiction. | Mystery and detective stories.
Classification: LCC PZ7.1.S569 Mar 2019 | DDC [Fic]—dc23 LC record available at https://lccn.loc.gov/2018041572

Printed in Canada

Published by Pelican Publishing Company, Inc.
1000 Burmaster Street, Gretna, Louisiana 70053
www.pelicanpub.com

Contents

Acknowledgments 5
Part One: The Crime
The Victim: Comma 9
Part Two: The Interrogation
Suspect Number One: Period. 13
Suspect Number Two: Question Mark 17
Suspect Number Three: Ellipsis Points 21
Suspect Number Four: Left and Right Parentheses 25
Suspect Number Five: Apostrophe 29
Suspect Number Six: Hyphen 33
Suspect Number Seven: Opening and Closing Quotation Marks 37
Suspect Number Eight: Colon 41
Suspect Number Nine: Exclamation Point . . 45
Suspect Number Ten: Semicolon. 49
Suspect Number Eleven: Em and En Dash. . 53
Part Three: The Conclusion
Conclusion. 58
What it All Means (the jobs of our suspects) . 60
Some Other Nifty Factoids 63

9
8
7
6
5
4
3
2
1
0mm

Acknowledgments

Endless love to the one and the three, my most important boys. Endless affection to Marilyn, Dan, and Kirsten—couldn't have done this without you. Endless appreciation to Nina, Devinn, and Christina for your talent and belief. Dora and Erin, you deserve much thanking, too. To all who have touched this book in any way, thanks and thanks and thanks.

Part One:

The Crime

POLICE DEPARTMENT

Punctuation County

MISSING

COMMA

LAST SEEN YESTERDAY
AT RECESS

The Victim: Comma

The Crime: Yesterday afternoon at approximately 1:17 p.m. the victim went outside for recess. It was a typical afternoon; no shifty sorts or unsavoury personalities were seen lurking around the schoolyard. Comma—a known busybody—was outside with all the other marks . . . until he wasn't.

Possible Reasons for Abduction: Comma has trouble listening to rules. Sometimes he shows up when he's not needed. Other times he doesn't show up when he's supposed to! People often use him in the place of other marks. This sometimes makes the other marks angry. Who could be angry enough to mark-nap him though? That is what we must find out.

Objective: We must interrogate all the punctuation marks that were out with Comma that day and identify the perp. Your job is to help me decipher clues and to use logic to figure out who has committed the crime before it's too late and Comma disappears forever.

Whenever you see a **bolded word** with a tiny number (that tiny number is called a superscript, Sidekick), flip to the back of the book and find the matching number for some more nifty factoids about it!

Part Two:

The Interrogation

9
8
7
6
5
4
3
2
1
0 mm
Punctuation County
Sheriff's Dept.
004

Suspect Number One: Period

"If you ask me (which you should of course) Comma is not needed. Why use a comma when you could just start a new sentence? Others are capable of doing stuff around here too you know! Has anyone asked *me* what *I* think? No. They haven't. Oh . . . that's what you're doing right now? Okay. Go ahead then."

—Period

Fact

Period has one job **and**[1] one job only: to end a sentence. Without him sentences would become long and unwieldy and well just hard to read plus they'd go on and on and on forever and ever without a stop and you wouldn't be able to quit reading a book until you'd read the entire thing because if Period weren't there it would just be one really really really super long sentence. Fortunately for us Period is here.

Detective: What exactly do you do?

Period: Oh[2]**.** Hi. I'm so glad you asked. It's about time someone took notice of me. I mean yes I'm small but that doesn't mean I'm *invisible!* It just so happens that my job is the most important of all. Without me you'd all be *so confused.* You would be. Trust me. Sure Exclamation Point can end a sentence . . . and Question Mark . . . and Em Dash. And I suppose Ellipsis Points too. But none of them do it with my finesse. I mean look at how tidy I am! I'm delicate. Dainty. Like a freckle on the face of a princess. Like a mole on the bum of a unicorn—oh. Did I say that out loud?

D: A freckle . . . with a unibrow? Okay . . . Well I guess that's not important right now. What *is* important is this: where were you at the beginning of recess yesterday afternoon?

P: Excellent question. Everyone should be more interested in my whereabouts at all times. I am simply that interesting. I was—oh. I can't remember.

D: Are you aware of any reason another mark may wish to harm Comma?

P: Heavens me! Are you suggesting there may have been . . . foul play? Do you think Comma has been . . . erased?

D: Just answer the question please.

P: Certainly. There are other less . . . *conservative* marks shall we say that have always been envious of Comma. You know. Some marks jump into Comma's place when they shouldn't. That's whom you should be questioning.

D: Can you provide any names?

P: Well I hate to point fingers but . . . *it was Exclamation Point!* There. I said it.

D: And what leads you to believe that?

P: All I'm saying is that I don't *not* believe it was her. Plus she's always taking the place of other *perfectly suited* marks. Take my job for example. Exclamation Point thinks she can do it just as well. She's always jumping in to end a sentence.

D: Are there any other marks that you think may have been involved?

P: Well there's always that irksome fellow Question Mark. Never in my *life* have I met a mark more nosy—wait! Where are you going? Don't you want to ask me more about myself? I may have seen something without realizing how important it is!

   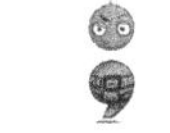    

Detective Work

Okay trusty Sidekick. Now is when I need your help. Period told us some of his uses as well as some that belong to the other marks. Did anything seem amiss to you? Does Period have anything to gain by stealing Comma?

Does he:
Have **motive?**[3]
O Yes
O No

Hide out in the background often popping up in places he doesn't belong?
O Yes
O No

Seem the suspicious sort?
O Yes
O No

Status:
What is your gut telling you?
O Guilty
O Not Guilty

Wait . . . I think someone else is waiting to talk to us. Let's turn the page and find out who it is.

9
8
7
6
5
4
3
2
1
0 mm
Punctuation County
Sheriff's Dept.
007

Suspect Number Two: Question Mark

"Wait what? Are you talking to me? Why on *earth* would you suspect me? Do you have issues? How do I know you're not covering *your own* shifty behaviour? Well? *Are you?* Where were *you* yesterday during afternoon recess? Hmm? *Hmm?*"

—Question Mark

Fact

Question Mark is the most inquisitive of all the punctuation marks. Not only does he always ask questions but he never answers one without asking something in return. He is a moderately well liked mark but his suspicious nature is what has made him suspect number two.

Detective: What exactly is your function?

Question Mark: What do you mean?

D: I mean in common English writing mechanics what do you do?

QM: Why do you want to know?

D: I'm trying to run an investigation here. Could you please just answer the question?

QM: What's in it for me?

D: There is nothing in it for you Mr. Greedy! Your friend is missing and I thought—

QM: What makes you think Comma is my friend?

D: Well . . . isn't he?

QM: Shouldn't you be asking more intelligent questions like: What? When? Where? How? And Why?

D: I'll run my investigation how I want. Quit changing the subject! You do realize that by refusing to answer my questions you're making us even more suspicious.

QM: Was that a question?

D: *Do you see a question mark at the end of it?*

QM: Exactly. I don't see one there and I didn't see one at the end of recess yesterday afternoon. Ask anybody. I simply wasn't there. Will that be all?

D: . . . I suppose.

Detective Work

I admit that I'm a little frustrated. Trusty Sidekick I am depending on you to keep your cool and help me figure out the clues. All that we learned about Question Mark—aside from his rather irritating tendency to answer a question with another question—is that he likes to evade interrogation. That makes me suspicious. What do you think? Does Question Mark have motive to want to mark-nap Comma?

Does he:
Have the ability to do Comma's job?
O Yes
O No

Hide out in the background poking his nose into places it doesn't belong?
O Yes
O No

Seem the suspicious sort?
O Yes
O No

Status:
What do you think Sidekick? Is he:
O Guilty
O Not Guilty

Wait . . . do I hear snoring? Who the *heck* could be sleeping at a time like this? Now *that's* suspicious behaviour if I've ever seen it. Let's flip the page and **find out who it is.**[4]

9
8
7
6
5
4
1
0 mm
Punctuation County
Sheriff's Dept.
0010

Suspect Number Three: Ellipsis Points

"Please call me Ellipsis P. No need to . . . spell out my whole name every time. Now where was I? Ah yes. I was under a tree having my pre-snack snack (a raspberry jam and salsa sandwich—*magnifique!*) when suddenly . . . it was as if someone had come up and just removed a part of the sentence! Usually I am . . . notified of such things. So you can imagine . . . my level of concern!"

—Ellipsis Points

Fact

Ellipsis P. is used far too often. People tend to get her use confused with Semicolons Em Dashes and Commas. Sometimes it's hard to tell her apart from her identical twin sister **Suspension Points.**[5] But Ellipsis P. has her own special job. Let's talk to her and find out what it is. And most importantly where she was yesterday at recess.

Detective: Would you explain your job to us please?

Ellipsis P.: Oh an interview! I feel like a contestant on Jeopardy! I'll take "Crime and Punishment" for two hundred Alex!

D: No one is being punished yet miss. We really just want to get to the bottom of the mystery. So if you don't mind . . . your job?

EP: Oh yes! Of course. Silly me. Where's my head? No . . . seriously. Where's my head? Sometimes it rolls away.

D: Uh . . . we should get back to—

EP: Ah here we are! Sorry about that. Okay well mostly my job is to . . . inform others that words have been taken away. You know . . . from a quote or something. Sometimes when people have too much to say it's best to . . . get to the point! Know what I mean? Blah blah blah—bor-ring! Ellipsis Points—awe-some. I'm sort of a . . . place marker.

D: And it appears you can also act as a long pause just like Comma. And you can end a sentence when dialogue trails off. What I mean is we spoke to Period earlier and he said—

EP: Oh that guy. You shouldn't believe a word he says. It's my identical twin Suspension Points who can end a sentence not me—folks get us confused all the time. And Suspension Points couldn't possibly have mark-napped Comma. Her alibi is airtight. She was sleeping as usual.

D: Oh! And where is Suspension Points now?

EP: Why she's right over there having her pre-nap nap of course. I can vouch for her whereabouts yesterday afternoon. Everyone can (she snores super loudly! We all heard her).

D: Ah. Okay.

EP: Besides she is too slow to do any mark-napping—always spreading things out. She and I couldn't be more different. I think we should all just get a little closer . . . we should . . . hug more. Close up . . . gaps. Bring it in for a huddle like a football team.

D: We could do that but I don't see how it will bring Comma home any faster.

EP: I do. If we'd spent yesterday afternoon in a big group hug . . . no one could have been mark-napped. It'd have been like creating a big old . . . punctuation chain of peace and love! "All we are sayin' . . . peace a chance" and all that.

D: Right. So do you ever jump in and take Comma's place when you know you're not supposed to?

EP: Me? No way. I take things out. I don't add extra stuff in.

   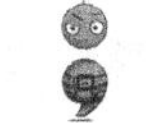    

Detective Work

Okay, so for someone whose job it is to *remove things* from a sentence Ellipsis P. seems rather uninterested in taking Comma's place. Still is it possible she removed Comma by accident while she was removing other things? What do you think trusty Sidekick?

Does Ellipsis Points:
Have the ability to do Comma's job?
O Yes
O No

Creep around in places uninvited?
O Yes
O No

Seem the suspicious sort?
O Yes
O No

Status:
What do you think this time?
O Guilty
O Not Guilty

I don't mean to alarm you Sidekick but I think I hear a disturbance of some sort on the next page! I hope you're done with your assessment because we *need* to get over there!

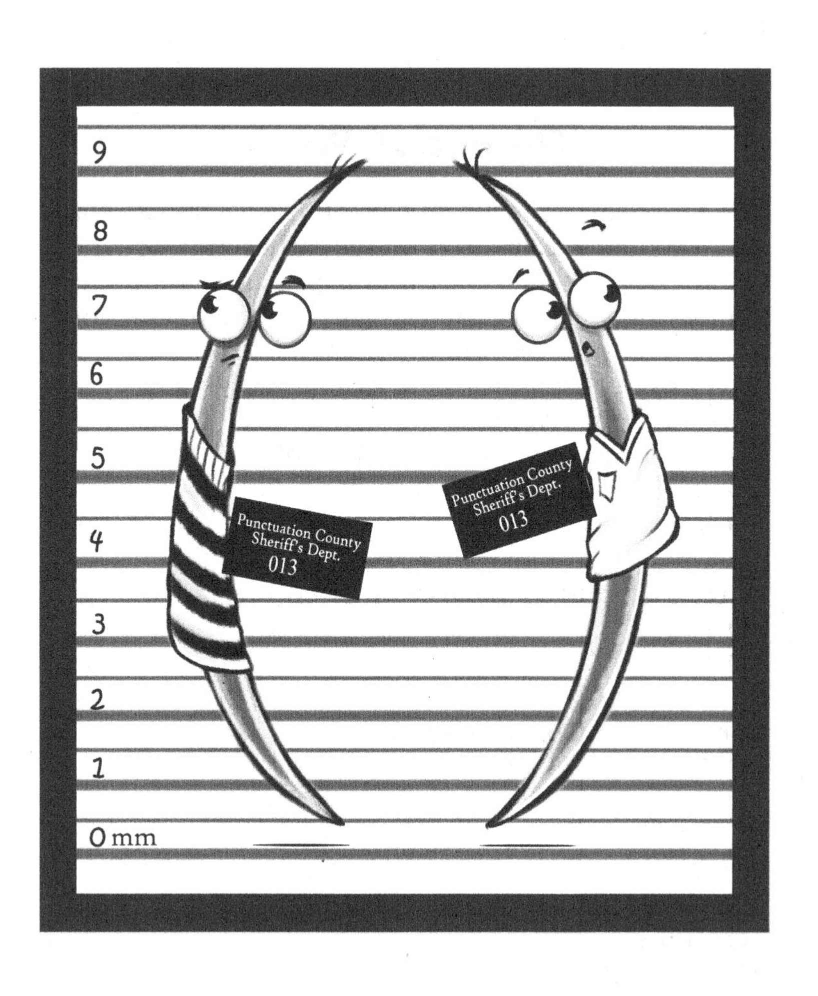
9
8
7
6
5
4
3
2
1
0 mm
Punctuation County
Sheriff's Dept.
013
Punctuation County
Sheriff's Dept.
013

Suspect Number Four: Right and Left Parentheses

"Hey you. Yeah you. Come here. We have something to tell you. But you can't tell anyone. (Not even your best friend and definitely not your parents.) It's a secret-like. Got it? Not. Another. Soul. *Capisce?* Okay here it is: A rabbit a donkey and a fish walk into a bar . . ."

—Right and Left Parentheses

Fact

Right and Left Parentheses don't go anywhere alone. Wherever you find one you can be sure the other is lurking nearby. They love to tell secrets and gossip and are always adding extra bits of information and stuff into otherwise complete sentences. When they're used too often they can be confusing. Their secretive nature is what makes them suspect number four.

Detective: All right boys. No funny business. Got it?

Right and Left: Got what? We don't got nothin'.

D: (Hmm . . . They're jokesters. That's what I was afraid of.) (Wait! Why did my thoughts just appear on the page like that? As if they were an additional aside to my sentence! I'd better watch what I think!)

R and L: Oh yeah. Feels good to get out into the open all you want to say doesn't it? Don't tell anyone but before we became Parentheses we thought of becoming counsellors.

D: Is that so?

R and L: Yep. We really believe it's best to just speak your mind.

D: Hmm . . . (And here I thought these two were the troublemaking sort.)

R: Troublemaking? Nah. Well . . . there was that one time with En Dash and the Whoopee Cushion . . .

D: Um . . .

L: Shhh! You're not supposed to say anything about that. But . . . remember the time we stole Exclamation Point's megaphone and hid it under Suspension Points' bed?

D: Boys . . .

R: And remember when we convinced the Quotation Marks that they had no voice?

D: Boys!

L: Oh yeah! That was a gas!

D: *Boys!*

R and L: Gee whiz! You don't have to yell!

D: So it seems (extremely!) obvious that you two like secrets and you like a bit of fun. The question is this: are you capable of taking Comma's place in a sentence?

R and L: (What should we say? Sometimes we *do* take Comma's place. But that doesn't mean we're guilty!) Okay so we like to interrupt sentences and add extra information sometimes or whatever. That's kind of our job (you know someone says a thing but we *all know* it's not all that they have to say). So yeah we can do one of his jobs. But *we didn't mark-nap comma!*

R: We didn't.

L: Nope.

Detective Work

I don't know what to think around those two! There is no question—they're a bit mischievous but does that mean they're capable of mark-napping? Trusty Sidekick let's go over the facts.

Do Right and Left Parentheses:
Have the skills to do Comma's job?
O Yes
O No

Like to sneak around?
O Yes
O No

Seem suspicious?
O Yes
O No

What's your Gut telling you Sidekick?

Are they:
O Guilty
O Not guilty

Did you hear that Sidekick? Someone just screamed! It sounds as though someone just stole something! Let's go see what all the hubbub is about.

9
8
7
6
5
4
3
2
1
0 mm
Punctuation County
Sheriff's Dept.
016

Suspect Number Five: Apostrophe

"Hey out of my lab! Everything you see in here is *mine!* Don't touch. In fact everything you *don't* see is mine too. And so is everything you have. And—wait! My latest experiment is . . . is . . . waking up! *It's alive!*"

—Apostrophe

Fact

Apostrophe is a mad scientist. Sometimes her experiments are successful but other times they're just . . . weird. She likes to remove things from the bodies of words and add the leftovers together! A real horror show! We'd better be careful around her S'kick—Oh no! She got you too!

D'tective: I heard someone scream a moment ago. Could you explain what happened please?

Apostrophe: Oh sure. I was just standin' next to the words "can" **'n'** [6] "not" enjoying a spot of fun—totally innocent o' course—when suddenly . . . Say d'you need that left ear o' yours? It would look smashing attached to this letter "t."

D: Um . . . moving on . . . So do you do that often? Take things I mean?

A: Sure sure. But no one minds. I mean look at all o' me wonderful creations! I'm a scientist . . . like Dr.

Frankenstein! *Way* more skilled than that horrible Hyphen character the big know-it-all. *Ahh! There he is!*

D: Why don't you like Hyphen?

A: Isn't it obvious? I'm a true master o' the craft—a word joining artiste—he's a hack! He joins words together too a'right but not with my finesse. We used to be friends but then—

D: What's the strangest word you've ever created?

A: The most beautiful word of all: Shouldn't've.

D: Wow. That's quite a mouthful!

A: Yeah. Isn't it great? I also make words that end in "s" both plural and possessive. Not everyone can say *that*—Oh look! There are "it" and "is" strolling next to one another! I'll . . . be right back. Don't. Touch. *Anything!*

Detective Work:

Wow. Apostrophe is a little bit . . . did you see all those mutations and creations! It's creepy. Okay S'kick what do you think about Apostrophe?

Is she:
Able to do Comma's job?
O Yes
O No

Sneaky?
O Yes
O No

The suspicious sort?
O Yes
O No

What's your gut telling you s'kick?
O Guilty
O Not Guilty

What's all that mumbling? It's as if someone is saying one really *really* long word. It's so hard to understand! Let's go check it out.

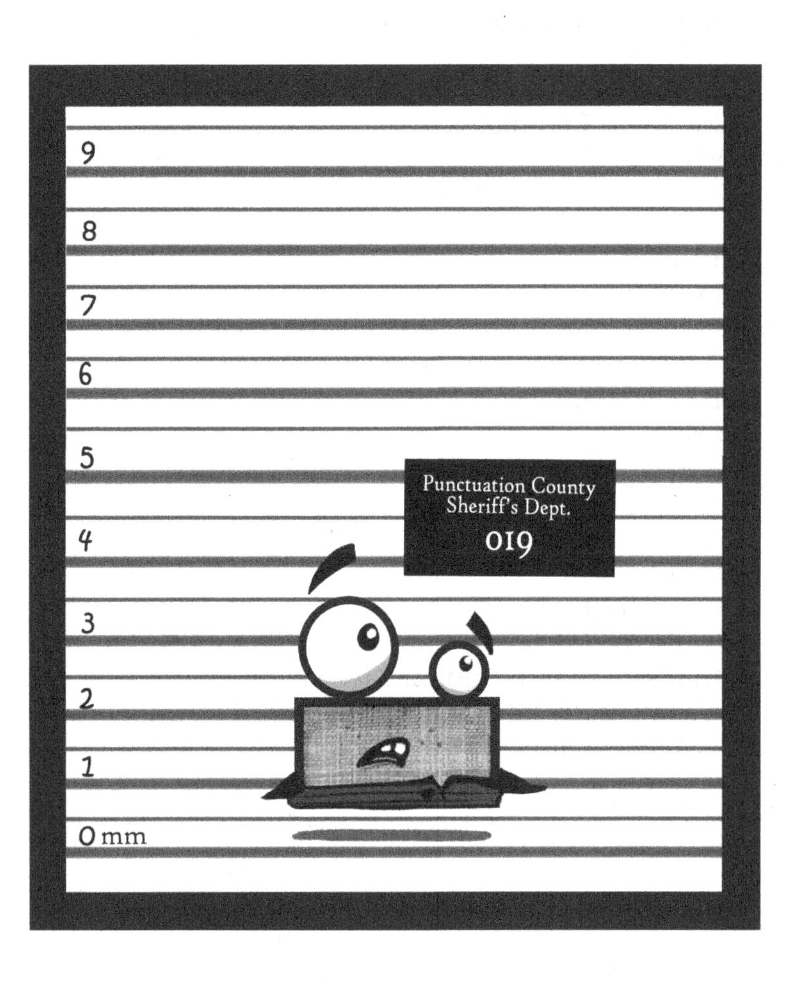
9
8
7
6
5
4
3
2
1
0 mm
Punctuation County
Sheriff's Dept.
019

Suspect Number Six: Hyphen

"Well-I-see-you-already-talked-to-Apostrophe-the-big-whiner. She's-just-jealous-because-I-am-so-much-more-creative. I-mean-look-at-the-fabulous-super-long-words-I-can-make! Plus-she's-a-thief. I-don't-take-things. I-stick-them-together. Except-those-horrible-"ly"-**adverbs.**[7] Awful-creatures!"

—Hyphen

Fact

Hyphen is kind of easy to confuse. He often jumps into the place of Em or En Dash without realizing it! He's the shortest member of the Dash family and he has his own distinct jobs. His easy-to-confuse nature is what makes him suspect number six.

Detective: Wow for being such a small character you certainly are capable of making long words!

Hyphen: Yeah. Isn't-it-great?

D: I suppose. It's also a bit confusing. Do you have rules to follow?

H: Probably-but-I-don't-know-them. Something-to-do-with-nouns-and-adjectives-and-stuff. Like-if-two-words-are-stuck-together-to-describe-a-noun-I'm-supposed-to-jump-in. If-the-describing-words-come-after-the-noun-I-don't-do-anything. I-think-I-should-just-attach-everything-though!

D: Do you have any other jobs?

H: Sure! Sometimes-when-a-super-long-word-comes-at-the-end-of-a-line-of-text-I-hop-in-there-so-the-read-er-knows-that-what-follows-is-still-a-part-of-the-word. It's-called-a-"soft-hyphen."

D: Do you know who might want to mark-nap Comma?

H: Sorry-Coach. I-don't.

Detective Work

I don't know. Hyphen doesn't seem like the mark-napping sort and he doesn't seem to be all that interested in doing Comma's job. But as we both know it's often the ones you don't suspect who are guilty. What do you think?

Does Hyphen:
Have the skills to do Comma's job?
O Yes
O No

Like to creep into places all sneaky-like?
O Yes
O No

Make you suspicious?
O Yes
O No

What's your gut telling you?
O Guilty
O Not Guilty

Whoa! Who's yelling! Sounds like a fight in progress! Maybe we should call for backup! Or maybe we should just go and check it out.

9
8
7
6
5
4
Punctuation County
Sheriff's Dept.
021
3
2
1
0 mm

Suspect Number Seven: Opening and Closing Quotation Marks

"Let me speak!"
"No *you* let *me* speak!"
"No *me!*"
"No *me!*"
"Okay. Let's both speak."
"*Good idea!*"
—Opening and Closing **Quotation Marks** [8]

Fact

Opening and Closing Quotation Marks are actually best friends though you'd never know it from listening to them! All they want to do is talk talk talk all the time; it's impossible to get a word in edgewise. We'll have to do our best with these two Sidekick. Their pushy nature is what makes them suspect number seven.

Detective: Can you please tell us where exactly you two were yesterday at afternoon recess?

Opening and Closing: Sure! We were in Public Speaking class!

O: We're going to be famous when we get older you know.

C: Yeah. Everyone *loves* to hear us talk!

O: I kind of want to be a carnival barker.

C: But I want to be president!

O: But we decided—carnies!

C: No! President!

O: Well I'm not going. You'll have to be the president without me.

C: That's not fair! I can't go anywhere without you!

O: Well I guess you'd better reconsider then!

D: Hey Opening and Closing? Are you able to do Comma's job?

C: No *you'd* better reconsider!

O: Okay okay. How about talk show hosts instead?

C: Hmm. That has possibilities. Let's—

Detective Work

Sidekick we're not going to get anywhere here. It seems obvious that all Opening and Closing Quotation Marks are capable of doing is talking. Let's—

Opening: *Hold it!* That's not true!

Detective: It's not?

Closing: No! We can also add emphasis to words.

O: Yeah. Those are called "scare quotes." Hey Closing do you remember when we—

D: Is that the only other thing you can do?

C: Nope!

D: Nope?

O: Nope! We are also used to format titles of short works or parts of longer works. Like newspaper articles and stuff.

C: We're also super good on the debate team!

O: Do you want to hear us—

Detective Work (Part Two)

Okay Sidekick. Let's examine the facts to see if these two should remain on our suspect list.

Are Opening and Closing Quotation Marks:
Capable of doing Comma's job?
O Yes
O No

The kind of marks that pop into places without anyone noticing them?
O Yes
O No

The sneaky sort?
O Yes
O No

What do you think? Are they:
O Guilty
O Not Guilty

Whoa! Did you hear that? I think I hear a drill sergeant on the next page! I didn't know this was a military school! I guess we'd better go see what's up with that.

9
8
7
6
5
4
3
2
1
0 mm
Punctuation County
Sheriff's Dept.
021

Suspect Number Eight: Colon

"It's like this: I'm not guilty. This is simple to understand if you consider the following facts: 1) I never really hang out with Comma 2) Comma's jobs are different than mine and 3) I really like lists too."

—Colon

Facts

Colon is known for being really organized. He likes his shirts crisp and his bed sheets tucked in. If what he said in his statement is true—the part about his like for lists—is it possible he snatched Comma to totally *own* list making? This question is what makes him suspect number eight.

Detective: Tell us more about your appreciation for lists please.

Colon: Look at it like this: I like numbered lists because numbers are a lot of fun.

D: Yes. And?

C: Here's another thing: I also like bulleted lists because bullets are almost like little pictures and I can sneak them into books that are not supposed to have pictures.

D: So you're sneaky then?

C: Look at it this way: I believe everything should have a proper introduction. I like to announce what I'm going to do before I do it. Does that sound sneaky?

D: Hmm . . . I suppose not. But would you ever be in the position to do Comma's job?

C: Does Comma do any of the following: 1) keep introductions separated from their lists 2) indicate the beginning of a block quote 3) Occasionally separate a tag from dialogue?

D: Yes!

C: He does?

D: Well he likes to organize lists. And he often separates a tag from its quote.

C: You've misunderstood me. It's like this: I don't like to organize the *elements inside* the list. I like to keep the introduction separate from it. It's not hardly the same thing.

D: No. I suppose you're right.

C: And then there's this: I rarely ever keep tags from their quotes anymore. I used to do it lots back when that fine fellow **Shakespeare**[9] was writing. But nowadays I prefer the finer things. Like introductions. There's nothing like a good introduction.

Detective Work

Hmm . . . I don't know what to think. Sidekick this one may take some extra sleuthing. Colon said he likes some of the same things that Comma likes but that their jobs are not the same. What do you think?

Does Colon:
Have a reason to want to mark-nap Comma?
O Yes
O No

Often sneak into places without being noticed?
O Yes
O No

Make you feel suspicious?
O Yes
O No

What do you think this time?
O Guilty
O Not Guilty

I had no idea punctuation could be so loud! How many of the marks that we've met so far have been yelling? Well the next one certainly is no exception! Let's put in some earplugs and go check it out.

9
8
7
6
5
4
3
2
1
0 mm
Punctuation County
Sheriff's Dept.
027

Suspect Number Nine: Exclamation Point

"Hi! I'm so happy to meet you! I'll be glad to answer any questions you have for me! And any questions you might have for the other marks too! Oh I just *love* to answer questions!"

—Exclamation Point

Fact

Exclamation Point is always excited and doesn't let anything get her down—which is why she's cheer captain! She makes sure every pep rally has all the pep it needs—and more! Pep rallies make her happy. Like really happy. Like so happy she could just *explode!* Was she so excited that she stepped in where she wasn't supposed to? That's what we must find out!

Detective: Can you explain what you do for us please?

Exclamation Point: Oh I'd *love* to!

D: Excellent. When you're ready then.

EP: Where should I start**!?**[10] I do *so* much!

D: Um . . . just the basics. What do you do?

EP: Oh that's easy. I bring joy!

D: What do you mean?

EP: Rainbows and unicorns! Oh I just *love* rainbows and unicorns. Don't you!?

D: Well yes I suppose. Everyone loves unicorns.

EP: And ice cream too!

D: Right. But I don't really see how that's relevant to—

EP: You know who *really* likes ice cream?

D: No but I really think we should get this conversation back on tr—

EP: *Comma!* He just *loves* ice cream! Almost as much as I love rainbows and unicorns!

D: Is that so?

EP: Yes! Isn't that just the funniest thing you've ever heard!?

D: Well no. Not really.

EP: What is then!?

D: Well earlier today we were questioning Right and Left Parentheses and they told this joke about a rabbit and a donkey and a fish—Wait! This is not at all the way the conversation should be going!

Detective Work

Okay Sidekick I admit that I got a little distracted. So much energy in one room makes my head spin! I need your cleverness to sort this one out. What do you think?

Is Exclamation Point:
Capable of doing Comma's job?
O Yes
O No

Always sneaking into places she doesn't belong without being noticed?
O Yes
O No

The suspicious sort?
O Yes
O No

What do you think Sidekick? Is she
O Guilty
O Not Guilty

Hmm . . . This is strange Sidekick. I don't hear anything. Who could be being so quiet? Sounds like whoever's in the next room is one sneaky character! Let's go see who it is.

9
8
7
6
5
4
3
2
1
0 mm
Punctuation County
Sheriff's Dept.
030

Suspect Number Ten: Semicolon

"If I were to mark-nap anyone it would be Period; you don't need to end a sentence when you can just use me instead; if all your clauses are closely related I can separate them just as well—like I have in this perfect specimen here[.] (← optional)."

—Semicolon

Fact

Semicolon is the trickiest of all the marks. He is forever being used incorrectly. I hadn't really noticed him sitting in the background all quiet-like until now Sidekick. Some people are afraid to use him and others use him when he shouldn't be used. Let's get to the bottom of this shifty character.

Detective: Can you explain your jobs to us please?

Semicolon: I could if I wanted; I dislike talking about myself.

D: How about just one of your jobs then.

S: Nope.

D: Hmm . . . Is it because Comma has become more common than you these days?

S: He may be more common but he's not as strong.

D: What do you mean?

S: I mean if Comma were a street cat by comparison I'd be a lion.

D: You're that strong?

S: Like a superhero; I'm thinking of making a costume. So far all I have are my red underwear a purple belt and a pair of orange socks. I'm working on a helmet though.

D: Sounds cool.

S: You don't know the half of it! Did you know that I can keep **independent clauses**[11] together *without* the help of a conjunction?

D: Really?

S: Yeah. I can also sort out really complicated lists that Mr. Wimpy Comma can't manage on his own.

D: What kind of lists?

S: Oh ones with other punctuation inside and stuff.

D: Can you show us?

S: Sure. When I'm a superhero I will be able to 1) fly 2) see things that are invisible and 3) have super back scratching abilities; a) correct punctuation b) grammar and c) spelling errors; and i) eat tacos ii) fish sticks and iii) cucumbers.

D: Wow that *is* a super skill to have.

S: I know. And Comma thinks he's the only one who can handle lists.

Detective Work

I have a sneaking suspicion about Semicolon sidekick. He seems to be feeling a bit bitter that Comma is more common than he is. Is that motivation enough for Semicolon to want to mark-nap Comma though? What do you think?

Does he:
Have the ability to do Comma's jobs?
O Yes
O No

Sneak into places without being noticed?
O Yes
O No

Seem the type that might mark-nap Comma?
O Yes
O No

What does your gut say this time Sidekick?
O Guilty
O Not Guilty

Shhh . . . Do you hear that? Squabbling! I mean not a fight but hushed whispering. Who could that be? Let's turn the page and find out.

9
8
7
6
5
4
3
2
1
0 mm
Punctuation County
Sheriff's Dept.
033

Suspect Number Eleven: En and Em Dash

"Poor wee speck little Comma is. All missing and alone. He's so tiny! I'm always telling my cousin En that size doesn't matter since he's much smaller than I am but between us I don't know if that's true. I never get confused with a hyphen like poor En does for example. That's because of my size—I look nothing like Hyphen! Being big has its advantages. Still we're both equally as important and we both have important jobs to do. But you know how little cousins can be. Now En quit pouting and come over here. Have a cookie and settle in. The nice detective has some questions for us."

—Em Dash (with En in the background somewhere)

Fact

En and Em Dash are kind of hard to tell apart. En is the width of a capital letter "N" and Em is as wide as a capital letter "M." The mother hen of the schoolyard Em is always picking up when others can't finish their work. En is a bit quieter with only a couple of jobs of his own. Let's talk to them and see what their jobs are and if they should remain on our suspect list or not.

Detective: Mmm . . . These cookies are delicious!

Em: Thank you dear. Chocolate chip—as well as oatmeal and snickerdoodle—are En's favourite kind of cookie too.

En: Em's always baking 10–12 batches per week!

D: That's a lot of cookies! I wonder why you're not plumper.

En: Are you calling me small? Why I oughtta—

Em: No no no! Of course he's not dear. (En is very sensitive being a smaller mark than I am.)

D: I wasn't! I was just saying that if I had that many cookies I'd be eating them all the time.

En: They are rather delicious. On a scale of 1–10 I'd rate them a 12.

Em: Oh you . . .

D: Could you explain your jobs for us please?

En: Certainly. I love to watch sports and keep track of the scores. I like to indicate a range too. Sometimes I help out my cousin Hyphen when he needs to connect words that are already connected.

Em: And I . . . well . . . I don't do much.

En: Don't be bashful Em.

Em: All right. Let's see . . . I sometimes add parenthetical elements to sentences.

D: Go on . . .

Em: I can step in if Comma or Semicolon are busy and act like a super comma.

D: And . . .

Em: Sometimes if someone is suddenly interrupted I break the sentence by—

D: And that's all the time we have. Thank you for your help.

Detective Work

Sidekick I have a case of cookie brain! Sounds as though Em is not as innocent as she lets on. What do you think?

Do En and Em:
Have motive to want to mark-nap Comma?
O Yes
O No

Often sneak around and hide where they don't belong?
O Yes
O No

Seem kinda sketchy?
O Yes
O No

This is it. For the last time Sidekick are Em and Em:
O Guilty
O Not Guilty

Well I think that's everything. Let's turn the page and study the facts.

Part Three:

The Conclusion

Conclusion

Now that we've heard from all our suspects it's time to make our decision. You've been a great help all this time Sidekick and I just can't solve this crime without you. Using your answers from our interrogation let's think this through logically. That should help us reduce our suspect list until we find our answer.

First let's figure out who has the motive to want to mark-nap Comma. Sidekick who is able to do Comma's job?

Most Motivated:
1)
2)
3)

Next let's decide who are the ones most likely to sneak into a place where they're not supposed to be. Write your answers here:

Sneakiest Suspects:
1)
2)
3)

And finally sometimes our bellies can tell us a whole lot. Sidekick which of the marks gave you the heebie-jeebies? Maybe they were dishonest or short tempered. What do you think?

Sketchiest Suspects:
1)
2)
3)

All right! Now we're getting somewhere! Now tally up the suspects. Do you have any that were repeated on two lists? Do you have any that made an appearance on all three? Sidekick do you know who our perp is? *Well please tell me!*

The mark-napper is:

Wait . . . Did you say . . . *ice cream?* Comma's mom bought Rocky Road ice cream so Comma went home during recess to have some? You mean . . . there is no mark-napper amongst us? Comma is perfectly fine? He's just taking a really long pause? Oh thank heavens! I knew I could count on you Sidekick!

Now about that missing Rocky Road ice cream . . .

What it All Means
(the jobs of our suspects)

Functions of the Period:
- To end a sentence. Period.

Functions of the Comma:
- To separate elements in a list of three or more items
- To separate independent clauses when used with a conjunction
- To separate an introductory word or phrase
- To separate optional parenthetical phrases
- To separate coordinating adjectives
- To separate a tag from a quote
- To separate a phrase from an independent clause if the phrase comes first
- To separate elements in a date or address
- To separate digits in a large number
- To indicate a pause in thought or speech

Functions of the Question Mark:
- To indicate the end of a question

Functions of the Ellipsis:
- To indicate missing text from quoted material
- To indicate trailing or stuttering speech

Functions of the Parentheses:
- To allow for additional information or thoughts to be included within a sentence that may not fit the flow of or may not be as important as the sentence proper but that you want to get in there anyway

Functions of the Apostrophe:

- To indicate missing letters or numerals from a word or number by creating contractions
- To indicate a possessive
- To indicate a plural possessive

Functions of the Colon:

- To indicate the beginning of a list when the words that come before it make a complete sentence of their own
- To (sometimes) separate an introduction from a quote
- To indicate the start of a block quote
- To introduce an idea that has further explanation

Functions of the Hyphen:

- To create temporary compound words or numbers especially when those words or numbers are followed by a noun

Functions of Quotation Marks:

- To indicate the beginning or end of speech
- To indicate the title of a short story poem or song; single chapter article or essay taken from a longer work
- To (rarely) provide emphasis to a word (these are called *scare quotes*)

Functions of the Semicolon:

- To separate two independent clauses that you want to keep in the same sentence
- To help sort out a monster list especially when the list contains other punctuation
- To act as a "super comma" if a regular comma seems too weak
- To be added before the word "however" or "foremost" or others of the sort that occur mid-sentence.

Functions of the Exclamation Point:

- To provide emphasis to a sentence
- To express excitement or another strong emotion

Functions of the En Dash

- To indicate a range
- To join words that are already joined by a hyphen

The Function of the Em Dash:

- To act as a "super comma"
- To indicate a parenthetical addition
- To indicate a sudden halt in speech
- To indicate something has been left out when joined together (usually a name in a legal document or a bad word that we don't want to write or something like that)

Some Other Nifty Factoids

1. *Conjunctions* are super awesome super sticky words with several important jobs. They can join independent clauses together, but only if they're used with a comma! Sometimes they can take the place of commas and keep things moving along and still make sense and be grammatically correct. . . . But doing that can make sentences really long and difficult to follow. And conjunctions can start a sentence, but should only be done occasionally and for a specific purpose. Conjunctions are For And Nor But Or Yet So. That's right—*FANBOYS!*

2. Sometimes sentences can be made up of only one word. Often these are *interjections* in dialogue. Here are some examples of one-word sentences: Stop! Wait! Go! No. Oh. Okay. Yes. Why? What? Where? How? Who? How many one-word sentences can you find in this book?

3. *Motive* means you have a reason to do something. It may not be a good reason—like stealing your brother's stinky old socks because all of your clean ones are under the bed and you don't feel like bending over to get them—but still . . . a motive is a motive.

4. A "phrase" is the part of a sentence that does not have a noun and a verb, and ***does not make sense on its own.*** In this nifty factoid, the clause is **bold** and the phrase is ***italicized.*** The conjunction joins them together. No comma is needed with the conjunction when the clause comes first.

5. *Suspension Points* look exactly the same as ellipsis points, but their function is a little different. While ellipsis points are used to show where words have been taken out, suspension points are more about the way a thing is said or read. And that thing is usually slow and . . . drawn out. Like . . . if you need time to . . . think of the right word. That's when you will want to call on your friend Suspension Points.

6. Two words that have been stuck together without a hyphen (like *cannot* and *handout* or when letters are actually removed like *it's* and *they're*) are called *contractions*, but in some spoken dialects words are routinely shortened—even ones that aren't contractions (like 'o rather than "of").

7. An *adverb* is a word that describes a verb (an action word). A lot of adverbs end in "ly" but not all of them. Some "ly" adverbs: happily, sleepily, softly, heavily, cheerily, and sadly. You will almost never see Hyphen attaching a word to one that ends in "ly." I think Hyphen is afraid of those letters.

8. In the United Kingdom, people often use single *quotation marks* for indicating dialogue. The opposite is true for people in North America. When a quote is used within another quote, things can become complicated!

9. *William Shakespeare* was (and still is) a super famous playwright and poet that lived from 1564 to 1616. When you read his works, which you will likely have to do in secondary school (warning: there's kissing in some of them!), you may think they were written in a different language. Some of the punctuation usages were different then than they are now, too, such as the use of Colon.

10. Sometimes Exclamation Point and Question Mark team up and create what is called an *interrobang*. Not too many people like the interrobang, but it is sometimes used in fiction novels—especially those for kids. It is meant to add emphasis to a question. It looks like this: !?, ?!, or ‽.

11. An *independent clause* is the part of a sentence that has a person, place, thing, or idea (a noun) and an action (a verb) and makes sense on its own. Most complete sentences are independent clauses. This sentence is an independent clause. **The bolded part of this sentence is an independent clause,** but ***the italics part is not.*** Check out factoid **4** about phrases for more information.